Things I Learned in
Second Grade

Amy Schwartz

KATHERINE TEGEN BOOKS

An Imprint of HarperCollinsPublishers

The titles *Superfudge* (© 1980),
Fudge-a-Mania (© 1990), and *Double Fudge* (© 2002)
by Judy Blume are used by permission of Dutton Children's Books,
a division of Penguin Young Readers Group,
A Member of Penguin Group (USA) Inc.,
345 Hudson St., New York, NY 10014,
and also by permission of Bodley Head,
an imprint of The Random House Group Ltd.,
20 Vauxhall Bridge Road, London SW1V 2SA.
All rights reserved.

Things I Learned in Second Grade
Copyright © 2004 by Amy Schwartz
Manufactured in China by South China Printing Company Ltd.
All rights reserved.
www.harperchildrens.com

Library of Congress Cataloging-in-Publication Data
Schwartz, Amy.
Things I learned in second grade / Amy Schwartz.— 1st ed.
p.   cm.
Summary: A young boy shares all of the things he learned and
how he changed in second grade, what he still wonders about,
and what he hopes to accomplish when he is in third grade.
ISBN 0-06-050936-8 — ISBN 0-06-050937-6 (lib. bdg.)
[1. Learning—Fiction. 2. Schools—Fiction.] I. Title.
PZ7.S406Th 2004   2002155507
[E]—dc21   CIP
AC
Typography by Stephanie Bart-Horvath
1 2 3 4 5 6 7 8 9 10
❖
First Edition

When I started second grade,
I couldn't spell "should."

I couldn't subtract 348 from 411.

I couldn't write in cursive.

Or read a chapter book.

Or play a xylophone.

When I started second grade,
I wasn't friends with Joseph.
Or William or Tommy or Sam or George.

Now I am.

When I started second grade,
I was friends with Ryan.

But now I'm not.
He's always trying to be Einstein.

Before Ms. Jones's class,
I had never heard of

a conflict resolution committee.

Or *Double Fudge*
or *Superfudge*
or *Fudge-a-Mania*.

Or Thomas Edison

or George Washington

or Albert Einstein

or Beezus and Ramona.

When I began second grade,
I lived with Mom and Dad and Princess.

Then we got Digger.

Then I lived with Mom and Dad and Princess
and Digger.
And Tiger,
and Explorer,
and Speedy,
and Racer.
They all came to school on Pet Day.

Would anyone like a hamster?

In the second grade
Dad picked me up
on Mondays and Wednesdays.

Mom picked me up
on Tuesdays and Thursdays.

And my sitter Alice picked me up on Fridays.
Sometimes she would bring her son.
I've known Alex since I was one.
He's my oldest friend.

Once, when I was two, I couldn't stop crying.
Mom couldn't cheer me up.
Alice couldn't cheer me up.
Then Alex walked by with a cookie on his head.
I stopped crying.

Alex is in the fourth grade.
He has a hamster now.

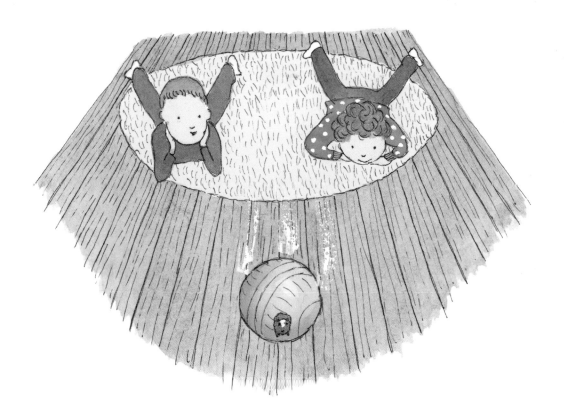

Moths dream about sweaters.
Z dreams about becoming A.
Kids dream about everything.
Markers dream about paper.
Grownups dream about being kids
again.

That's a poem I wrote
in the second grade.

Here are some pictures I drew.

This is Anger.

This is Happiness.

This is William.

This is Joseph.

These are the aliens invading earth and
there's a giant battle and it's the
Civil War and the aliens blow up the
earth and we attack with blastoid asteroids
and that's the end.

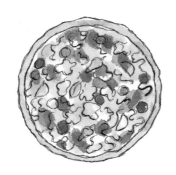

If an asteroid blew up the dinosaurs,
how did the earth survive?
What is bubble bath made of?
What is in everything pizza, anyway?
Should I try sushi?
How do you draw a lion walking?
How do his legs go?
Do you know?

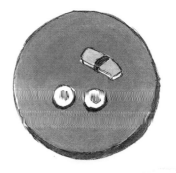

Today I graduated from second grade!

I can spell

If 203 boys want ice-cream sandwiches, but 163 ice-cream sandwiches melt in the sun, how many boys get ice-cream sandwiches?

I know the answer.

Andrew Henry Smith

I wrote that.

Charlie and the Great Glass Elevator.
Beezus and Ramona.
Captain Underpants and
  the Attack of the Talking Toilets.
I read those.

I was mayor of the class.
I resolved conflicts.

I built a lot of towers.
I did a lot of science.

I kicked a lot of soccer balls.
I made a lot of friends
in the second grade.

Have you ever built an Iroquois museum?

Or been a little Lincoln?

Or read a whole Harry Potter book on your own?
I'm going to do all that . . .

in the third grade.
See you then!